To Deseronto Public Library,

Ruowen Wang

Little Joy

Story by Ruowen Wang
Illustrated by Wei Xu

Kevin & Robin Books Ltd.

To all adoptive and foster parents:
The heart has enough room for everyone;
may yours be filled with love and laughter.

Published 2008 by Kevin & Robin Books Ltd.
http://www.kevinandrobinbooks.com

To contact the publisher or to request permission
to make copies of any part of the work,
please visit Kevin & Robin Books Ltd. online for further information:
www.kevinandrobinbooks.com

Library and Archives Canada Cataloguing in Publication

Wang, Ruowen, 1962–
Little Joy/Ruowen Wang, Wei Xu.

ISBN 978-0-9738799-7-1 (bound)

I. Xu, Wei, 1967–
II. Title.

PS8645.A534L47 2008   jC813'.6   C2007-904497-2

Little Joy
Kevin & Robin Books Ltd.

First Canadian Edition 2008
Printed and bound in Hong Kong, China

Little Joy is a sweet baby.
She smiles all the time.

Little Joy's mother is a very happy new mom,
or almost very happy, except for one thing....

Little Joy never laughs,
no matter what people do
to try to make her.

Mommy tickles Little Joy on her big toe.
Little Joy smiles, but does not laugh.

Mommy tickles Little Joy on her knee.
Little Joy smiles, but does not laugh.

Mommy tickles Little Joy on her palm.
Little Joy smiles, but does not laugh.

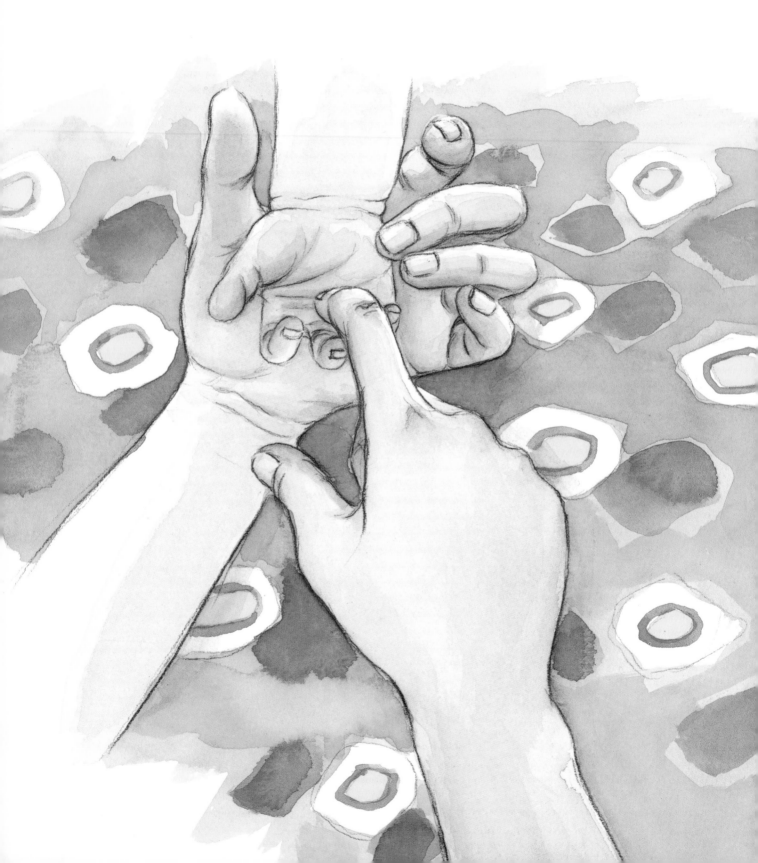

Mommy tickles Little Joy on her tummy.
Little Joy smiles, but does not laugh.

Mommy tickles Little Joy on her chin.
Little Joy smiles, but does not laugh.

Mommy tickles Little Joy on her nose.
Little Joy smiles, but does not laugh.

Mommy tickles Little Joy on her ear.
Little Joy smiles, but does not laugh.

Mommy tickles Little Joy's hair.
Little Joy smiles, but does not laugh.

Now Mommy is about to cry.

Little Joy tickles
Mommy's hair.
Mommy smiles,
but will not laugh.

Little Joy tickles Mommy on her ear.
Mommy smiles, but will not laugh.

Little Joy tickles Mommy
on her nose.
Mommy smiles,
but will not laugh.

Little Joy tickles Mommy on her chin.
Mommy smiles, but will not laugh.

Little Joy tickles Mommy on her tummy.
Mommy smiles, but will not laugh.

Little Joy tickles Mommy on her palm.
Mommy smiles, but will not laugh.

Little Joy tickles Mommy on her knee.
Mommy smiles, but will not laugh.

Little Joy tickles Mommy on her big toe.
Finally, Mommy laughs out loud,
and with such a funny melody!

Suddenly, Little Joy bursts into big laughter.

Little Joy's laugh makes Mommy laugh even more.
Little Joy and Mommy laugh and laugh and laugh ...
and they haven't stopped laughing ever since.